The Hopi

by Natalie M. Rosinsky

Content Adviser: Bruce Bernstein, Ph.D., Assistant Director for Cultural Resources, National Museum of the American Indian, Smithsonian Institution

Reading Adviser: Rosemary G. Palmer, Ph.D., Department of Literacy, College of Education, Boise State University

COMPASS POINT BOOKS
MINNEAPOLIS, MINNESOTA

FIRST REPORTS

Compass Point Books
3109 West 50th Street, #115
Minneapolis, MN 55410

Visit Compass Point Books on the Internet at *www.compasspointbooks.com*
or e-mail your request to *custserv@compasspointbooks.com*

On the cover: Hopi Katsina Brown Badger by C. Torivio

Photographs ©: John Elk III, cover; Photo Network/Michael P. Manheim, 4–5, 25; Greg Probst/Corbis, 6; George H. H. Huey/Corbis, 8; Bob Rowan/Progressive Image/Corbis, 9; The Denver Public Library, Western History Department, Call Number X-30818, 10; The Denver Public Library, Western History Department, photographer Sumner W. Matteson, Call Number X-30767, 11; The Denver Public Library, Western History Department, photographer John K. Hillers, Call Number X-30828, 12; Library of Congress, 13; Tom Bean/Corbis, 14, 16, 18, 23; The Denver Public Library, Western History Department, Call Number X-30864, 17; The Denver Public Library, Western History Department, Call Number X-30774, 19; Colorado Historical Society, 20; Charles Sanders/Visuals Unlimited, 21; Smithsonian American Art Museum, Washington, D.C./Art Resource, N.Y., 24; Photri-Microstock, 26; Courtesy Museum of New Mexico, neg. #11409, 28 (top); Hulton/Archive by Getty Images, 28 (bottom); Stock Montage, 29; Mary Evans Picture Library, 31; Northern Arizona University/Special Collections and Archives, 32; Bethel College, 33, 34–35; Corbis, 37; Courtesy Jack Lankhorst, 38–39; Frank Staub/Index Stock Imagery, 40–41; AP/Wide World Photos/Daily Times/Penny De Los Santos, 42–43; John Cross/The Free Press, 48.

Creative Director: Terri Foley
Managing Editor: Catherine Neitge
Photo Researcher: Svetlana Zhurkina
Designer/Page production: Bradfordesign, Inc./Les Tranby
Cartographer: XNR Productions, Inc.
Educational Consultant: Diane Smolinski

Library of Congress Cataloging-in-Publication Data
Rosinsky, Natalie M. (Natalie Myra)
  The Hopi / By Natalie M. Rosinsky.
    p. cm. — (First reports)
  Includes bibliographical references and index.
  ISBN 0-7565-0641-7 (hardcover)
  1. Hopi Indians—History. 2. Hopi Indians—Social life and customs. I. Title. II. Series.
  E99.H7.R63 2005
  979.1004'97458—dc22   2004000590

Copyright © 2005 by Compass Point Books
All rights reserved. No part of this book may be reproduced without written permission from the publisher. The publisher takes no responsibility for the use of any of the materials or methods described in this book, nor for the products thereof.
Printed in the United States of America.

Table of Contents

Who Are the Hopi? 4

Wise Farmers 8

Family and Village Life 11

The Fourth World 16

A Year of Dances 20

Arts and Crafts 24

Explorers, Settlers, and Missionaries 26

Soldiers, Settlers, and Missionaries 29

Further Change and Growth 34

The Hopi Today 38

Glossary 44

Did You Know? 45

At a Glance 45

Important Dates 46

Want to Know More? 47

Index 48

NOTE: In this book, words that are defined in the glossary are in **bold** the first time they appear in the text.

Who Are the Hopi?

The Hopi (pronounced HO-pee) are a native people of the American Southwest. Today, there are more than 11,000 members of this tribe. About 10,000 Hopi live on their **reservation** in northeastern Arizona. It is located near where the states of Arizona, New Mexico, Utah, and Colorado meet. It is surrounded by the Navajo Nation. The other 1,000 Hopi live outside the reservation.

Hopi means "peaceful," "wise," or "well-behaved ones" in the language of the Hopi people. While the Hopi share some **customs** with another Southwest native people, the Pueblo, their languages are different. The Hopi language is one of a group called Uto-Aztecan.

▲ The Hopi village of Mishongnovi is perched high on Second Mesa in Arizona.

Hopi history tells us that this native people migrated to where they are now many millions of years ago. Non-Hopis who study the Hopi suggest that their ancestors were a basket making people called the Anasazi. They lived in this same dry area for more than 1,200 years. Their homes were pit houses. Then, about 1,300 years ago, the Anasazi began to build dwellings above ground. These houses were made of stone and hardened mud. Between the years 900 and 1100, the Anasazi grouped their homes close together. They built some on the high, rocky **mesas.** These houses became some of the first Hopi villages.

▲ *The ruins of a 12th century home rise above boulders in the Arizona desert.*

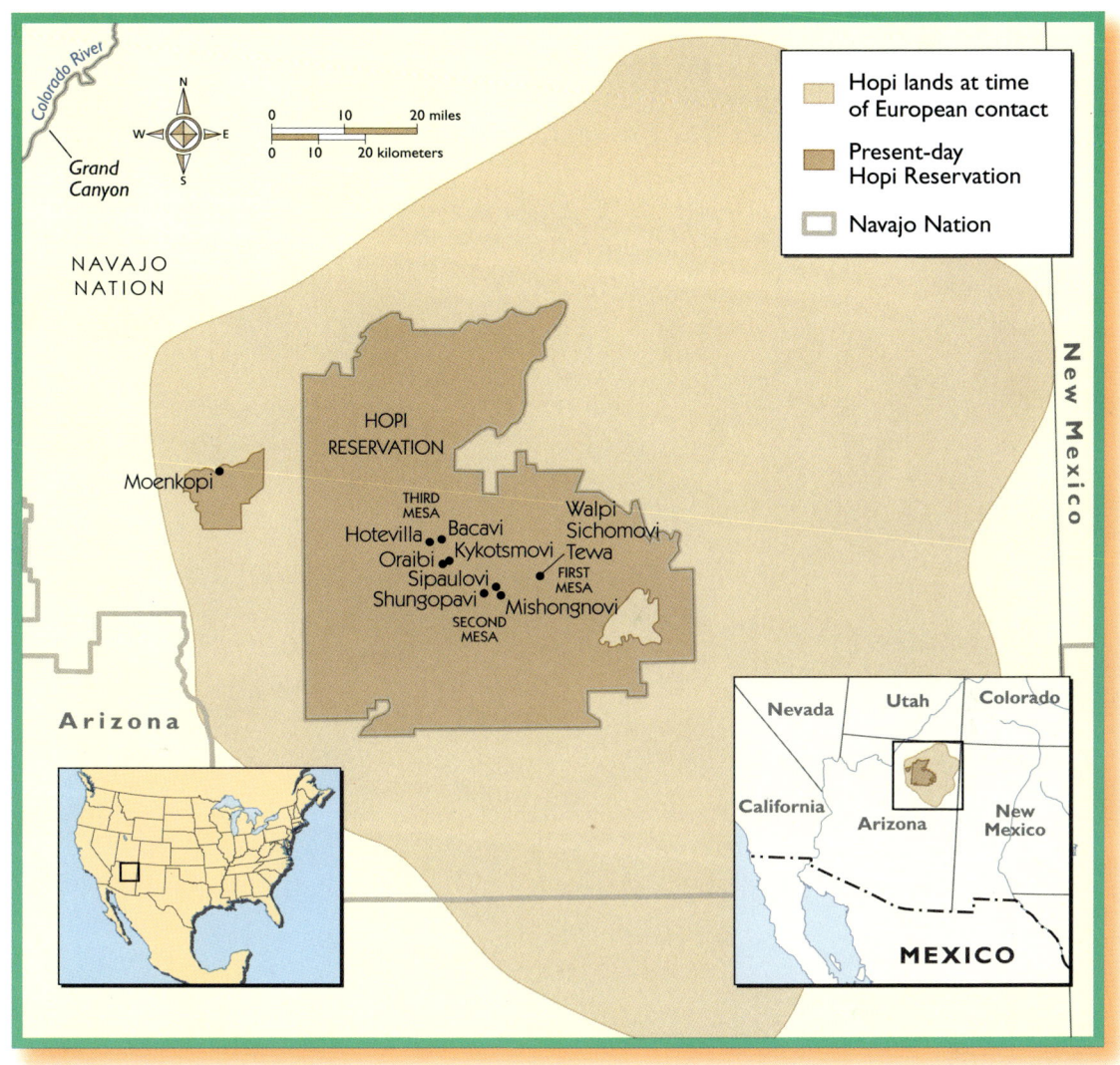

▲ A map of past and present Hopi lands shows the 11 villages on three mesas.

Today, there are 11 villages on the three mesas of the Hopi reservation. The Hopi village of Oraibi is the oldest continuously inhabited village in North America.

Wise Farmers

▲ A Hopi farmer works in his cornfield. The only water it receives is from rainfall.

The Hopi have a **tradition** of being wise farmers. Because there is little water in their area, the Hopi have always planted crops in ways that use every drop of rain. To keep moisture in the soil, they did not plow it. They dug only small holes to plant seeds or used large, flat stones to shield the soil from the sun's direct, drying rays.

▲ Corn in a traditional Hopi basket

The Hopi grew and ate many types of colorful corn, which led others to sometimes call them "people of the blue corn." The Hopi also grew beans and squash. They planted and ate fruit, too. Usually, men planted and harvested field crops, while women worked in the **terrace** gardens.

▲ Ladders reached the upper levels of homes as shown in this 1920 photo of Walpi.

The Hopi stored extra food in rooms inside their permanent homes. These stone buildings were held together with clay and wood. They could be several stories high. Ladders were sometimes used to reach the upper levels. The Hopi arranged their houses into villages surrounding a central open space. This community space was called the plaza.

Family and Village Life

In addition to taking care of the household gardens, women were responsible for all cooking. They ground corn into flour and made bread. A flat bread called *piiki* was popular. Women also wove strong, beautiful baskets from parts of the yucca plant. They made and decorated clay pots. Girls learned these jobs by watching and helping.

▲ *A girl with the traditional Hopi hairstyle weaves a basket in 1900.*

Besides farming, men wove cloth for blankets and clothing. At first, they used materials such as animal hair and pieces of wild plants. Later, they grew cotton for cloth. When Hopi men began to raise sheep, they used the wool for their weaving. A traditional dress called a *manta* was often made of woven black wool.

▲ A Hopi man weaves on a loom strung on a wall in Walpi on First Mesa in 1879.

Men also hunted deer, elk, and rabbits for food. Boys learned these jobs. When they weren't learning to work, children played games with marbles, sticks, and string.

▲ Edward S. Curtis photographed Hopi girls in 1906. Their hairstyles indicate their unmarried status.

In Hopi families, women owned the houses and land. When they died, this property belonged to their daughters. A family's heritage was traced through the mother's family membership, or **clan**.

▲ Ancient Hopi clan symbols are carved on a rock near Tuba City, Arizona.

When this clan grew larger, a family might build another story onto their house. At one time, there were 75 Hopi clans. A person from one clan could only marry someone from a different clan. The clans were also important to village life. Each clan identified with an animal, believing its members to be direct descendants of the animal.

Each village was independent. It had its own leader or head man in charge. This leader had to listen to the wishes of all the people in his village. He was helped by a **council** of clan leaders. They made certain that people and events followed the ways of the Hopi religion.

The Fourth World

The Hopi believe in several gods. According to the Hopi, a god named Maasaw made this world. It is the Hopi's fourth world. The Hopi believe they came here by climbing up through three other worlds. They arrived through a large hole at the bottom of the Grand Canyon. This spot, called the great **sipapu,** is a sacred place to the Hopi.

▲ A Hopi wall painting depicts a fertility god.

Hopi houses have special rooms called kivas, which include a sipapu. There, Hopi people learn about their religion. In the kiva, Hopi men also make clothing and objects for religious **ceremonies.**

Many of these objects show the spirit messengers of the Hopi religion. These "friends," or spirit messengers, are called katsinas. The Hopi prefer this spelling rather than the more common *kachinas*.

▲ *In this historical photo from the Denver Public Library, men enter a kiva for a ceremony in the late 19th century.*

The katsinas are said to carry Hopi prayers for good harvests, health, and rain. The katsinas bring food and gifts. They are also said to bring knowledge about ways to live a good, holy life.

There are more than 250 different katsinas. They take the form of animals or other natural creatures or things. Certain katsinas are of special importance to each Hopi clan. The Hopi sometimes make katsina figures. These dolls help Hopi children learn about their religion.

▲ *Hand-carved and painted representations of katsinas are given to children to help them learn about the many Hopi katsinas.*

▲ A Hopi katsina dancer poses in this historical photo from the Denver Public Library.

The Hopi believe they have been given a holy job. It is to help everyone as well as themselves. When they honor their gods and katsinas, the Hopi believe they are helping everyone in this fourth world.

A Year of Dances

The Hopi religion is connected to their life as farmers. Throughout the year, they pray for rain and good harvests. They also pray for the knowledge and strength to lead good lives. These prayers are part of ceremonies in which the Hopi dance. Sometimes, these dancers wear clothing and masks that remind them of different katsinas. The Hopi believe that the

▲ *Villagers watch a harvest dance in Oraibi in about 1900.*

▲ *Traditional Hopi dancers*

katsinas return to Hopi villages where people honor them through dances and ceremonies.

Each month brings different farming tasks. In the same way, each month has its own special, ceremonial dances. From January to July, there are katsina dances connected to planting crops. From late July through December, there are dances connected to harvesting crops. Different clans are most responsible for certain dances.

Dances often begin at sunrise. They may last for days. Some dances take place or begin in the kiva. Often, the Hopi dance through the plaza of their village. They also sing prayers.

Often during dances, order is maintained and proper behavior emphasized by a special type of dancer, known in English as clowns. They are not circus clowns, however, but very religious and important figures. The clowns, called mudheads and koshari, use humor to make points about proper and improper behavior.

In February, young Hopi children are excited to take part in the Bean Dance. They learn about the katsinas then. In the late summer, Hopi girls are happy when they are finally old enough for the Butterfly Dance. The dancers wear elaborately painted headdresses.

▲ A young Hopi girl is dressed for the Butterfly Dance.

Arts and Crafts

Like their ancestors the Anasazi, the Hopi make beautiful baskets and clay pots, which they decorate. Often, colorful katsinas, animals, and ceremonies are shown. Curved designs and repeated patterns are also used. Red, black, yellow, and white are traditional colors.

▲ Hopi women paint clay pots in this painting from the Smithsonian American Art Museum.

▲ A Hopi basket weaver

For many years, the Hopi made these things for their own use. When traders came to the reservation, they bought Hopi crafts. Then they sold them elsewhere. The Hopi began to make baskets and pots to sell to non-Hopis. Beautiful Hopi pottery has been collected by non-Hopis for more than 100 years.

The Hopi also show skill in the katsina dolls they make. Silver jewelry is another Hopi craft.

Explorers, Settlers, and Missionaries

▲ *Coronado came to the Southwest looking for gold.*

About 500 years ago, the Hopi way of life changed. In 1540, Spanish explorer Francisco Vásquez de Coronado arrived in the Southwest. Coronado and his soldiers met another Pueblo people, the Zuni, who lived in what is now New Mexico. The Spanish hoped to find gold, but failed. These soldiers brought horses to the area. The Spanish settlers who followed brought sheep, cows, goats, and pigs. They also planted fruit trees and different kinds of squash. The Hopi began to raise sheep and weave wool. They began to grow fruit and more vegetables.

These new customs did not arrive peacefully. Spanish soldiers destroyed Indian homes. They forced Indian women and girls to work for the settlers. Priests of the Roman Catholic religion had accompanied the settlers. These **missionaries** tried to force the Hopi to give up their religion. They hurt, and even killed, some Hopi.

In 1680, these peaceful people joined other tribes in a **revolt.** The Hopi and other Pueblo peoples fought the Spanish. For a while, they succeeded. In 1692, though, Spanish soldiers returned, this time led by Diego de Vargas. To escape, the Hopi left homes and sacred places in the valleys. They hid on the mesas and built more villages there. It took many years for peace to come. The suspicion and distrust of outsiders continues to this day.

▲ Diego de Vargas

▲ The village of Walpi was founded about 10 years after the revolt of 1680.

Soldiers, Settlers, and Missionaries

In 1821, Mexico became a separate country from Spain. Mexico controlled the Hopi and other tribes' land until 1848, when it lost a war with the United States. Then, American soldiers, settlers, and missionaries moved into the area. Some Navajos fought these invaders. The Hopi did not, yet many of the "peaceful people" still died. They caught a terrible disease called smallpox from their new white neighbors.

▲ Mexico lost a war against the United States.

Missionaries of several Christian faiths arrived. They tried to convince the Hopi to change their religion. Most Hopi did not.

In 1882, though, the Hopi way of life did change. The United States government established the Hopi Reservation. It only included about one-tenth of the Hopi's traditional land. According to the government, the Hopi no longer had a right to many of their sacred places. Instead, Hopi land was given to settlers or other tribes.

Although the Hopi had a successful lifestyle for more than 1,000 years, they were told to change. Their farming systems were well adapted for the dry climate of the mesas, but American farming methods were not. Yet the Hopi were told to use these new methods.

Other changes occurred that also hurt the Hopi. Many government officials did not respect Hopi traditions. They believed that Hopi children should learn the white man's ways. These children were

▲ *A woman fixes her daughter's hair in the traditional style. Government officials in the late 19th century did not respect Hopi ways.*

forced to leave their families and live in faraway schools. They had to speak English and were not allowed to speak their own language.

▲ Hopi and Navajo boys attended a boarding school in Tuba City, Arizona, in 1919.

They were even given new names! Because they missed their parents and families, many Hopi children ran away from school to return home.

▲ Hopi leaders were imprisoned on Alcatraz Island off the California coast.

Nineteen Hopi leaders refused to send their children to these schools in 1894. They refused to farm where U.S. government officials said they should. Early the following year, the men were put into prison on faraway Alcatraz Island in California for these so-called crimes. They were kept there for almost a year.

Further Change and Growth

Not all Hopi refused to change. This caused disagreement among the Hopi people themselves. A leader named Lololma was more willing to accept the white man's ways. He led a group that the U.S. government called the Friendlies. A leader named Lomahongyoma led the group that most resisted change. They were called the Hostiles. In 1906, this disagreement split the Hopi village of Oraibi.

▲ *Lomahongyoma (center, holding hat) led the group of Hopis called the Hostiles. They were imprisoned on Alcatraz Island.*

The Friendlies forced the Hostiles to leave Oraibi. The Hostiles then started new villages at Bacavi, Hotevilla, and Kykotsmovi. They made the village at Moenkopi larger. These villages continued to grow.

In 1936, the Hopi tribe grew in another way. Village leaders formed a tribal council. In the past, each Hopi village was self-governed and independent. Now all the villages would be governed by a single council and tribal chair. The council represented all the Hopi in matters involving the United States government.

▲ *Disagreements split the village of Oraibi in 1906.*

The Hopi Today

Today, the Hopi people are represented by their tribal government. Its elected officials deal with federal and Arizona laws that affect reservation life. These laws provide modern schools, health care, and other services to the Hopi. The tribal government also deals with businesses that are on Hopi land. The Hopi do not want mining companies to strip the earth or destroy sacred places.

▲ The village of Moenkopi is west of the main Hopi reservation and is part of Oraibi.

▲ *Traditional Hopi drummers and dancers*

The tribal government represents the Hopi in their argument with the Navajos. For many years, these neighbor tribes have disagreed about the

borders of their reservations. In 1974, the United States passed a law called the Navajo-Hopi Settlement Act. It solved some of these problems. Yet not every village supports the tribal government. The very traditional people of Oraibi choose not to be part of it. They refuse government services.

Tradition and religion remain important to most Hopi people. For this reason, they do not want katsina figures to be imitated. Some villages also no longer permit visitors to watch certain ceremonies.

There are now projects to save traditional knowledge and language. One project teaches the Hopi language in reservation schools. Another collects the stories of wise, old people. One of these elders, Dan Evehema, in 1996 spoke for the Hopi. He said, "Our prayer is to have a good happy life, plenty of soft gentle rain for abundant crops. We pray for balance on earth, to live in peace and leave a beautiful world to the children yet to come. … We are one after all."

As they grow as a modern tribe, the Hopi have not lost their traditional beliefs. They remain wise keepers of this "fourth world."

▲ Hopi elder Dan Evehema lived on and worked the same land for more than 100 years. He died in 1999 at age 108.

Glossary

ceremonies—formal actions to mark important times

clan—a group of related families

council—a small group of people that governs the whole group

customs—a group of people's usual ways of doing things

mesas—flat-topped hills

missionaries—people who travel to teach their religion

reservation—a large area of land set aside for Native Americans

revolt—an uprising by people who are unhappy with their rulers

sipapu—a small hole or indentation in the floor of a kiva

terrace—flat spaces on the sides of hills, mountains, or buildings

tradition—a custom that is common among a family or group

Did You Know?

- The Hopi produce 17 different kinds of corn—including three different shades of blue corn!

- A Hopi, Louis Tewanima, was a famous athlete. He won a silver medal for running the 10,000 meter race in the 1912 Olympics.

At a Glance

Tribal name: Hopi

Divisions: 34 clans, including the Katsina, Butterfly, Cloud, Crow Lizard, Bear Strap, Blue Bird, Eagle, Bear, Badger, Parrot, Snake, Puma, Rabbit, Bow, Spider, Snow, Horn, Sun Forehead, Reed, Corn, Sand, Rabbit Brush, and Coyote

11 villages: First Mesa villages: Walpi, Tewa, and Sichomovi; Second Mesa villages: Shungopavi, Mishongnovi, and Sipaulovi; Third Mesa villages: Hotevilla, Bacavi, Kykotsmovi, Oraibi, and Moenkopi (a satellite of Oraibi).

Past locations: 18 million acres (7.2 million hectares) of northeastern Arizona

Present locations: 1.8 million acres (.7 million hectares) of northeastern Arizona

Traditional houses: plastered stone and wood houses

Traditional clothing materials: woven cotton and wool mantas, belts, ponchos, breechcloths and shoulder robes, leather moccasins

Traditional transportation: foot, horse, and donkey

Traditional food: corn, beans, squash, melon, peaches, mutton, venison

Important Dates

700	First above-ground dwellings are built on Hopi land; corn is grown.
900–1100	Dwellings are grouped together to form the first villages.
1540	Francisco Vásquez de Coronado and his men explore the Southwest for gold.
1680	The Great Pueblo Revolt of the Hopi and other Pueblo people occurs.
1692	Hopi escape Diego de Vargas and his soldiers by hiding in the mesas.
1848	The United States wins the Mexican War and controls Hopi land.
1882	The Hopi Reservation is established.
1906	Hopi disagree about modern ways, and traditional Hopi move to other villages.
1936	Hopi Tribal Council is formed to deal with the U.S. government.
1974	Navajo-Hopi Settlement Act becomes U.S. law; an amended version is signed by President Clinton in 1996.

Want to Know More?

At the Library
Bierhorst, John. *Is My Friend at Home? Pueblo Fireside Tales.* New York: Farrar Straus Giroux, 2001.

Dawavendewa, Gerald. *The Butterfly Dance.* Washington, D.C.: National Museum of the American Indian, Smithsonian Institution; New York: Abbeville Press, 2001.

Secakuku, Susan. *Meet Mindy: A Native Girl from the Southwest.* Milwaukee, Wis.: Gareth Stevens, 2004.

On the Web
For more information on the Hopi, use FactHound to track down Web sites related to this book.

1. Go to *www.facthound.com*
2. Type in a search word related to this book or this book ID: 0756506417.
3. Click on the *Fetch It* button.

Your trusty FactHound will fetch the best Web sites for you!

On the Road
Hopi Cultural Center
P.O. Box 67
Second Mesa, AZ 86043
928/734-2401
To visit this museum and learn about events on the Hopi reservation

The Field Museum
1400 S. Lake Shore Drive
Chicago, IL 60605
312/922-9410
To see one of the largest museum collections of Hopi items and art

Index

Alcatraz Island, 33
Anasazi tribe, 6
baskets, 11, 24, 25
ceremonies, 17, 20-21, 24, 41
children, 11, 12, 22, 27, 30–32
clans, 13, 15, 21
clay pots, 11, 24, 25
clothing, 12, 17, 20
clowns (dancers), 22
corn, 9
council, 15, 36
dance, 20–22
education, 30–32, 38, 41
elders, 42
farming, 8–9, 20, 21, 27, 30
food, 9–10, 11
fourth world, 16, 19, 42
Friendlies, 34, 36
gods, 16, 19
harvesting, 21
Hostiles, 34, 36
houses, 6, 10, 13, 17, 27
hunting, 12
katsina figures, 18, 25, 41
katsinas (spirit messengers), 17–18, 19, 20–21, 24
kivas (sacred rooms), 17, 22
language, 4, 31, 41
mesas, 6, 7, 28, 30
missionaries, 27, 29, 30
Navajo tribe, 4, 40–41
Oraibi (village), 7, 34, 36
planting, 21
Pueblo tribe, 4
religion, 15, 16–19, 20, 22, 27, 30, 41
reservation, 4, 7, 25, 30, 38, 41
revolt, 27
settlers, 27, 29, 30
sipapu (sacred place), 16
Spanish exploration, 26–28
traditions, 8, 41, 24, 30, 42
tribal government, 36, 38, 40
villages, 6–7, 10, 15, 28, 34, 36, 41
weaving, 11, 12, 27
yucca plant, 11
Zuni tribe, 27

About the Author

Natalie M. Rosinsky writes about history, social studies, economics, science, and other fun things. One of her two cats usually sits on her computer as she works in Mankato, Minnesota. Natalie earned graduate degrees from the University of Wisconsin and has been a high school and college teacher.

2260

MAY - 5 2005